Muskrat
for Supper

D0709181

Muskrat for Supper

Exploring the Natural World
with the Last River Rat

Kenny Salwey

FULCRUM
GOLDEN, COLORADO

Text © 2012 Kenny Salwey

Photographs © Jack Lenzo/Fulcrum: i, iii, viii, xiv, 1, 2, 3, 5, 7, 11, 15, 22–23, 24, 25, 26, 29, 45, 47, 77, 80, 82, 105, 126, 144, 145; © Flickr Creative Commons and the following artists: 416style: vi; Randen Pederson: xi, 48; szatmar666: xiii; Mike DelGaudio: 9 (canoe); Richard Hurd: 9 (geese), 39 (sandhill cranes), 42; Kristopher Volkman: 18, 92; Andy Leeman: 19 (canoe); Phelyan Sanjoin: 19 (tree); Bev Sykes: 32; woodleywonderworks: 34; Janine and Jim Eden: 37; Peter Shanks: 39 (tree); Pierre-Selim: 51; John Benson: 52; Heather Katsoulis: 55; Ir3127: 56; Dave Langlois: 58; Karen Roe: 63; gailf548: 66; www.huntfishguide .com: 69; Andy Middleton: 72; Hugh Lee: 78; Martin Pettitt: 83; ted_rocket: 84; Paul Hamilton: 85; Jim Champion: 86; Gerry Thomasen: 88; Joshua Mayer: 91; West Point Public Affairs: 98; Ben Thompson: 100; Don DeBold: 102; Tom Brandt: 107; Danielle Scott: 110; Ben Dalton: 111, 114; nugefishes: 116; Col Ford and Natasha de Vere: 120; H Dragon: 125; Erich Ferdinand: 128; JelleS: 130; Walraven: 133; Dave & Margie Hill: 134; Tim Pierce: 137; Jeffrey Beall: 141.

All rights reserved. No part of this book may be reproduced or transmitted in any form or by any means, electronic or mechanical, including photocopying, recording, or by an information storage and retrieval system—except by a reviewer who may quote brief passages in a review—without permission in writing from the publisher.

Library of Congress Cataloging-in-Publication Data on file

Printed in the United States of America
0 9 8 7 6 5 4 3 2 1

Design by Jack Lenzo

Fulcrum Publishing
4690 Table Mountain Dr., Ste. 100
Golden, CO 80403
800-992-2908 • 303-277-1623
www.fulcrumbooks.com

To all children:
You are the only hope for the future wellness of
wild things and wild places.
May you always remain nature's child.

The natural circle of life turns slowly.
Life is too short to hurry through it.

Contents

A Note  from the Last River Rat

The following stories are all true. I have taken the liberty of creating some composite characters from the hundreds of schoolchildren and adults I have met, known, and talked with over the years, but in all cases, everything you read in this collection is based on fact, as well as my own recollections.

—Kenny Salwey

The Shack

On the banks of a backwater swamp along the Upper Mississippi River, the last river rat sits next to his shack. The dense woods surround him. As he looks out over the wetlands, there are no human sounds to interfere with the chirping of birds, the rustling of leaves, and the rippling of the water. The cool autumn air and the golden light of the shortening days make him wistful, and his mind turns to days gone by—being a kid, outdoor adventures, growing up, watching the world change around him. He smiles, remembering it all and mulling over which stories he'll tell.

Finally, he hears the soft muttering of a car making its way down the dirt road hidden by trees. The car appears around the bend, and the woodsman greets his visitors with a grin. They are adults now, with children of their own slamming the car doors, but in their faces he still sees them as kids: all smiles and dimples and inquisitive eyes.

"Been a long time," he says, sharing hugs.

"I'd like you to meet our kids," says the father. The young boy and girl say hi shyly as the river rat shakes their hands.

"Nice to meet you both. And welcome."

Noticing the small, odd skeletons hanging from the shack, the girl, wide-eyed, whispers her surprise in her brother's ear.

The river rat's eyes twinkle, missing nothing. "C'mon. I'll show you around..."

Welcome to my shack. Let me show you around. As you can see, I've gathered a lot of treasures over my years on the river. I'm not only a river rat; I'm a pack rat as well.

This here is a flathead catfish jaw, the lower jaw of a mud cat. They have no teeth; instead, inside their mouth it's like a rough sandpaper. It won't take your finger off. This one weighed forty-six pounds. And this is a towboat line. The loop is made without a knot. The connection is woven, making it very strong.

This here's a beaver skull. The beaver, of course, is the largest rodent in North America and the engineers of nature: they build dams out of sticks and mud. One of the few critters that can control its own environment. Yeah, they are very unique. Their two big front teeth are like a chisel. They need to chew to keep those teeth worn down. If they don't, the teeth would grow too long for them to eat, and that'd kill the beaver. They eat bark, and only bark. They cut a tree down to get at it.

This was a hollow tree that I cut down. I decided to make a toilet out of it and put a pail in there so it's legal. You can remove the pail, so it's not a traditional-type outhouse. I have two seats—one I keep by the stove in the winter so it's warm to sit on.

This is a handwoven net made by an old river rat. This is a skill that I never learned and I wish I would have, how to weave nets. You'll notice there are four knots on every one of those squares, so this is intricate work. However, just as people knit and watch TV at the same time, the old river rats could sit around and visit while they made nets. And this is a metal ring, so that when you put the net in the water it will sink under the fish rather than float on top. Just a little keepsake of bygone days, skills that have been lost and are gone.

This here is a snapping turtle shell. A snapping turtle has thirteen sections, or plates, on its shell. Every hard-shell turtle has thirteen parts to its shell: a painted turtle, a map turtle, a snapping turtle, a Blanding's turtle—they all have thirteen.

This is a horse skull. A Native American friend of mine—Smoky Jim Stokes, a Dakota

The Shack

Sioux—married my wife and I in a blanket ceremony, and we had a street preacher to make it all legal. Smoky Jim was a pipe carrier and a storyteller. The horse signifies the spirit of the wind on the earth. Its tail and mane flow in the wind. The red-tailed hawk circles in the wind, and it is the spirit of the wind in the sky.

Here is the front door, as it is. The sign says *La Maison de Salwey.* It's quite a house, using the term loosely.

So, this is Big Lake Shack. It's about thirty years old. It's made out of oak. It took the better share of a summer to build it, I would say.

The neighboring farmer had what they call home-sawed timber; there were no two pieces exactly alike. He let me take the lumber I needed. I nailed it together green, without drying it, because you can't get a nail in oak once it's dry. Then I got some waste oil, fifty gallons of it, and a paintbrush and painted it on the outside, and it bled right through the boards. That staining you see is the oil. Never did have to treat the wood again. One-time deal.

Yep. And that's the kitchen and that's the

dining room and that's the bedroom. So we've got a three-in-one here. The wood-burning stove keeps the place tolerable when it's twenty below. Just have to cut more dead wood to burn. Use only dead wood. I hate to cut a living tree to burn for firewood or for cooking, because they are so precious and it takes 'em forever to get big.

The great circle of life is all about respect. Respect and knowledge, learning about it. You can't love and respect something you don't know anything about. How do you do that? The very finest way, I believe, is actual outdoor experience. An outdoor experience evokes feelings, feelings produce attitudes and values, attitudes and values, in turn, create behavior. That's really what we are all about, I think—how we behave toward nature and the circle of life.

A River Rat Is Born

A crisp breeze picks up, and the group of friends wanders to the firepit and the campfire flickering there. The kids are drawn closer, holding their hands out to the small flames. Every now and then they look back at their parents in awe, as if asking, *You used to do this all the time?* The fresh air makes them feel alive and alert; they notice the squirrels playing in a nearby tree, the ducks puttering about across the water, the soft whistle of the breeze blowing through the woods. They listen intently as the river rat speaks of a time when he was their age.

The smoke drifts away on the homeless wind. The tales are spun...

I grew up not too far from the river. I went to a little one-room country school, chewed the covers off of books, made paper airplanes out of the paper. Went away at seventeen and joined the army. Ended up in Fort Dix, New Jersey. Went to New York City on a weekend pass—I was in culture shock. Perhaps the busiest place in the world, 42nd Street and Times Square. Slick little country bumpkin, standing, mouth hanging open, eyes the size of silver dollars, didn't know they made buildings that tall and that there was that many people in the whole world, let alone one town.

That's when it dawned on me that I should've been reading them books, should've been writing on that paper. I realized I missed something special and precious called *education*. My career opportunities were limited, so to speak.

So when my time was up, I came back to Buffalo County. I went into a place called Whitman Swamp and began to eke out a living the only way I knew how—the only skills that I knew were hunting, fishing, trapping, digging roots, collecting herbs. Some of my uncles were full-time river rats. My family was French Canadian; my father

farmed on a little farm in the hills, but still supplemented it with hunting and fishing and trapping.

Even though I had some outdoors skills, I still had a lot to learn. An old-timer would come along when I'd be out trapping in the winter and kneeling on that hard ice. He'd say, "Put a boat cushion in your sled. Kneel on the boat cushion, not on the hard ice. It's bad on the knees." I thought, *What does that old guy know?* By the time I was fifty-three, I had two artificial knees. But I did listen to the old-timers a lot. They were secretive. They didn't say, "Oh, come on son, I'll show you where you can catch the catfish; I'll show you where you can get lots of mink." You learn just by keeping the eating hole shut and the listening ones open.

Today, they call me the Last River Rat. That moniker, title, name was given to me when I wrote my first book, several years ago. Strangely enough, writers or authors a lot of times don't get to choose the title of their book—it's done by the editors or publishers, and I had no knowledge of that. In fact, I don't even type. I can't use a computer. I write in longhand and always will, because I'm computer illiterate by choice.

So I'll tell you, if I could, a little story about that, though there is no such thing as a little story when you are listening to a slow talker. However, when I began to write some columns for *Big River* magazine years ago, that wasn't the problem. It was a column; it wasn't a book. I could turn those in longhand and everything was hunky-dory, but when I decided to write a book, my wife, Mary Kay, said, "You got to learn how to use a computer here, Buster, because these people are not going to like it. It's probably been twenty-five years since they had a longhand manuscript dropped on them. So," she said, "there's a computer course at the local high school on Wednesday nights. You should go and learn how to learn to use a computer."

I said, "Well, okay, I'll give it a try."

Now, a little background. Sitting Bull was a famous Sioux war chief, medicine man, pipe carrier, an elder. When his people were "defeated," the government took him out on the prairie in South Dakota and said, "Don't worry about it. We will give you all this land out here. Look—you can't see the end of it. It is called a reservation; it will be yours, but you will have to stay there. We will teach you to be farmers, we will buy you these big horses instead of your Indian ponies, and we will buy you plows. Then we are going to build you little wooden houses, then you don't have to mess around with your big heavy teepees and moving them around all over."

So when the day came, the tribe moved to the reservation, and there was much crying and gnashing of teeth. The members of the tribe turned to Sitting Bull and said, "We don't want to be farmers; we want to hunt buffalo, but there are no buffalo left. We don't want to live in those little wooden houses; we want to live in our teepees as we always did. What shall we do?"

Sitting Bull said, "As you travel your new path of life, pick up what you come across, turn it over carefully in your hands; if it don't suit you, drop it like a hot rock." I always thought that was wise advice.

So, I went with Mary Kay to the computer class: one, two, three different nights, I guess. The fourth night I wasn't ready, and she said, "What's the matter?"

I said, "Computers are hot rocks. I don't want to use them."

Now, microwaves are good. I love microwaves. So I don't dislike all electronic gadgets. There is turning over things in your hand, the old and the new, you see.

I wrote my book, and the editor called me, and

A River Rat Is Born

he said, "We liked the book and we're going to call it *The Last River Rat*."

I asked, "What if I ain't?"

He said, "Well, we have something called poetic license." In other words, we can fib a little bit and get away with it. He said, "Furthermore, would anyone pick up that book if we called it, *One of the Last River Rats*?"

So that's how I got that name. River Rat—you earn that title; however, *The Last* is their concoction. But I have no doubt I am certainly one of the last. That lifestyle has simply disappeared, due to the fact that it will not sustain modern changes. It's all about simple finances. The best year I ever had as a river rat, in thirty years, I made less than ten thousand dollars—that's poverty level. However, it's not what you make, it's what you spend, and I spent very little and got by.

Today, younger folks end up being part-time river rats on the weekend and during vacation. However, to do it full-time is pretty much gone. That's happened before; change is constant. The mountain man era was short-lived, really, thirty-five years. But river ratting has been around for a long, long time. Whole families made a living as river rats. In every little river town along the Mississippi, there were fish markets and fur buyers.

So, that's the way it is, and I don't whine about it. Things have to change, and so as a way of life it's pretty much disappearing. At least it's not part of the circle of life disappearing. We will still be here, but we need to rearrange our way of living.

Exploring
the Natural World

The two kids share a glance.

"What do you mean by 'rearrange our way of living'?" the boy asks uncertainly.

"It's like I said before about nature and the circle of life—we can't appreciate and respect them unless we learn about them. You do that by going out and exploring."

"But we live in town," the boy says, "not out here on the river. How are we supposed to get all the way out to nature to explore it? I mean, we're not allowed to drive yet."

The river rat chuckles, not unkindly, and goes on...

Living with Nature

One can begin exploring the natural world in a very simple fashion—in your own backyard, even downtown in a big city, where there are some birds, there are ant colonies that one can watch, all sorts of critters big and small. Ants are one of the most amazing. They teach one the value of community, of working together. It's everybody working for the overall good of the colony, of the community. I think that is an important lesson that you can learn in any vacant lot. You can learn that sitting somewhere on a sidewalk that isn't quite put together right, and there's a crack there and some dirt—and there will be an ant colony.

To explore means to examine. There's a certain amount of adventure involved, and exploring the natural world is very simple. You don't need a lot of complicated or high-tech gadgets to do that. You can do that in your neighborhood by simply taking time to do it. Sitting down and listening. You learn that in the spring of each year, the birds return, and they all sing a different song, all in a different key, and they all sing at once. If we people did that, you couldn't stand it in here; however, in the natural world it's a beautiful chorus, and it's just good for a person—good for the spirit and the body, everything at once.

Everything that one needs to know about life, in general, can be learned from the natural world, pretty much. And there you start with a little handbook or field guide. Doesn't have to be fancy, just something that you can use to identify different critters and birds and trees and such. That is a part of your adventure.

As people get older, I guess some people tend to want to see grand vistas and faraway places; however, I believe that to explore in your own backyard, so to speak—let's say within even fifty miles of your house—is equally rewarding because there you get the four seasons in place. You get to see certain trees, ponds, creeks, or whatever in all four seasons of the year. You see that great change. And yet, the change occurs so gradually that it's sometimes almost impossible to notice it each day.

Walking Sticks

In addition to your own sense of adventure, you might consider a few items when exploring the outdoors. The first thing you should have is a walking stick. What good is a walking stick? A walking stick can't walk—however it does allow you to walk better. It's a third leg going up a hill; you can use it to test the depth of the mud or the water; you can use it for balance crossing a narrow ledge or a log over a stream; you can use it to pick up a rock or look under a plant without bending or stooping down to do it. But the big thing about walking sticks: you can hold them in your hand and lean on them and put them against your chest and stop. When you do that, you become more observant and more introspective. You will look inside yourself a little more.

To go afield without a walking stick means you are going to keep walking, for the most part; but with a walking stick, you will stop, and then you will see and hear—use all your senses—so much more.

Before long, that walking stick is a part of you. It's like a friend that can be made from all different kinds of wood—nothing fancy, and no sanding required. The sanding happens from your hands sliding up and down as you walk along. The oils and sweat from your skin soon make that walking stick nice and smooth and easy to handle. At that point, you can pick your walking stick out of twenty other ones, just by the feel and the height of it. A walking stick is invaluable, it's wonderful. Henry David Thoreau never set foot outside of his house without his walking stick; he called it *sauntering*, walking slowly and stopping often.

You begin with a small tree. One has to be careful, if you are on public land, about what kind of trees you can cut for making walking sticks or even for firewood. Generally, you want a walking stick that is just around your shoulder height, so once you have your small tree

cut, you nip it down to height. Then I use a knife
to carve my walking sticks. You always cut away
from you rather than toward you. What you are
doing is simply taking off the bark. There is an
inner bark and an outer bark. You want the outer
bark to be peeled off. If the inner bark stays on,
it will come off by itself through use. There's no
hurry—that's the nice part—when you are in the
natural world. What's the rush? Life is too short to
hurry through it!

When whittling a stick, one can pay attention to sounds and smells. If you have problems sitting still when you are observing and exploring, you can always whittle. Gives your hands something to do while you are sitting there. Just keep turning this stick, taking the bark off. It doesn't take long.

Possible Bags

The next thing you want is a possible bag. What's a possible bag? Well, its name is self-explanatory: everything you could think you might possibly need for a trip afield goes in your possible bag. Some of the finest possible bags I ever had were ladies' purses. Once you get over the idea of wearing a lady's purse out in the woods, there is nothing wrong with that. Any woman knows that it's not a purse, it's a possible bag. Everything you could possibly need, and much, much more goes into those purses. Right? I mean, it's amazing when my wife dumps out her possible bag—there is a mound of stuff!

Here is one of my possible bags. Not sure how old it is exactly, but I know it's more than fifty years old. It was made from a simple gunnysack, or burlap bag, and a short piece of rope. It is worn as a shoulder bag; that way, it is out of your way. You can swing it around to the back when you are going through the woods. A backpack is nice, but in a lot of ways it's cumbersome, and when you bend over, it's always wanting to flip over your head.

This one—I had a Native American friend make for me, many years ago. He tanned the leather and he put turtles on it—the turtle is my totem. When I go to schools, it will be sitting out on the table or something. I take a lot of different artifacts and talk about the circle of life and the place of each animal, and then, invariably, someone will say, "I bet that's blood." I say, "Sorry, no. It's chocolate milk." Spilled chocolate milk on it; that's why it's stained.

What do I carry in my possible bag? It depends on what I'm doing. Certainly a little pill bottle with some fish hooks and sinkers in there, just in case I might take a notion to fish, with some of that old black braided fishing line wrapped up on a little stick the size of a pencil. Of course, one of the standards is toilet paper. A lot of things have gone wrong for folks who have used leaves, especially poison ivy. Always a water bottle and a few matches in a watertight pill bottle. Pill bottles are great for that sort of stuff. During hunting time, I'd have a few .22 bullets along. You may want to have a small field guide of plants and animals and birds. The exploring is pretty much limited to those things, although, like I said, you see plenty of insects as well, maybe a cricket, maybe a grasshopper, ants, maybe a spider…so in that regard there is no real end to exploring the natural world.

Three Things

All of my life, wherever I go, I carry three special items: a jackknife, a magic rock, and a lucky penny.

A jackknife has a thousand uses, one of which is *not* a weapon. There are different names for them—penknife, folding knife—and most of them have more than one blade, and they are quite short bladed, maybe two inches at the most. You don't need a great big knife hanging at your side; when you have a jackknife, you have different styles of blades and uses. Always I carried a jackknife, even when I was a child, and no matter at school or wherever. If there was sometimes a disagreement over something, the jackknife stayed where it belonged—in my pocket. This whole idea of the paranoia, the fear of knives, comes about because of misuse. That is not what they are meant for. They are meant as a working tool. There's a small blade about an inch long that one can use to punch holes in things, maybe to put some rawhide string through some cloth. Always a knife should be as sharp as possible—a dull knife will cut you sooner than a sharp knife, because you put more pressure on a dull knife to get a job done, and that can turn into a point where maybe it slips for you. So, a dull knife is not good.

All rocks are magical in some way. I pick up

magic rocks all over the place. When one goes afield as a child, you come across an awful lot of things that are worth picking up and looking at.

That's one of the things that I think we lose when we become adults—that natural curiosity and the idea that one has to get right down there by the spider web in the grass, to touch it a little bit. Many times we adults just walk on by.

The magic rock can be any size. Of course, you want something that fits in your pocket or in the possible bag nicely, without taking up a whole lot of room. They can be any shape, any color, any size—the whole idea of a magic something is magic. Well, a rock will show itself to you sometimes when you walk along a beach or along a streambank, or it will almost jump toward you. It makes you look at it, and there is something magic about that. I like to pick those up and carry them with me. It's like picking up little jewels.

When it comes to a lucky penny, of course, it can be any penny—they are all lucky. They are lucky because they are worth the least of all of our coins, and yet they add up. I have found lots of pennies over the years, lying about outside on sidewalks or parking lots. I guess there are folks who drop a few pennies and don't even pick them up. I like the idea of a penny, because that way one is never broke. One always has a penny to one's name.

I also like to pick up little pieces of bark from trees, different kinds. In particular, birch bark, which is almost like writing paper and was used a great deal by Native people to build canoes, mind you, as well as to make dishes and eating utensils, things like that. Ash trees were used to make baskets—some of those baskets are just beautiful. These are old-time skills. I think that we should try to remember some of the old ways, because not all of the old ways are bad, and not all of the new ways are good.

We need to take some from each world, the new and the old, to make a better world. For instance, the canning of foods, which is a very old method of preserving food, is becoming more popular again. Now that we are rediscovering as we explore, we find certain things and say, "Hey, that's a good thing." The drying and smoking of meat is another example; there's a lot of people now smoking their own fish on a grill. They get these wood chips of hickory, cherry, or apple wood—that's another ancient way of preserving. When you think about the electricity it takes to run freezers as opposed to canning or smoking to preserve your food, the latter are so much more efficient. The whole idea of electricity, in some ways, amazes me—that we ever became so dependent on it.

Journals

When we are exploring the natural world, we will want to record what we see and hear, what our experiences are. One of the better ways to do this is with a journal. Why? Because it's simple. Along with your journal, you need only a pencil. A pencil is the best because you can sharpen the thing—if you run out of ink with a pen, you are kind of out of luck. I would recommend a small notebook of some sort, something that fits in your possible bag or in your pocket real comfortable. Find a quiet time to sit down and recall what you have seen and experienced that day. Then jot it down. It doesn't have to be poetic. You don't have to be a writer, you don't have to have some sort of eloquent sayings. All you need to do is just jot down: "I saw the most beautiful blue jay." Describe its colors a little bit, and how it scolded you as you walked through the woods, how the blue jay is sort of the town crier of the woods. They announce that there is something not right, that there is something going on in the woods. How do you feel about that blue jay? Is it worth seeing? Or experiencing? Will you ever see it again? Just short little things, whatever comes across your mind. You can, if you have an artistic bent, draw a picture. They say that a picture is worth a thousand words. Or maybe just write *blue jay* and the date—that's a good start.

Or you can keep a journal in your mind as well, then share it in discussions with other people through storytelling or just simply relating what the experience was about and why it's worth remembering. Your journal entries, at the times you are writing them, don't seem to be all that important; however, if you are able to keep them, five, ten years down the road, it's just wonderful to open those up, to relive outdoor experiences.

I always did keep a journal, even when I was a full-time river rat, for almost thirty years. I got these old bank calendars. Back then, they had huge squares for each day. They were big calendars. I would jot down notes each day, usually in the evening when I would come back from whatever I was doing. I would sit by the fire and just write a couple sentences describing what I did, what the weather was like, if I experienced something unusual. Otherwise just everyday things. "Oh, the wind blew just something awful

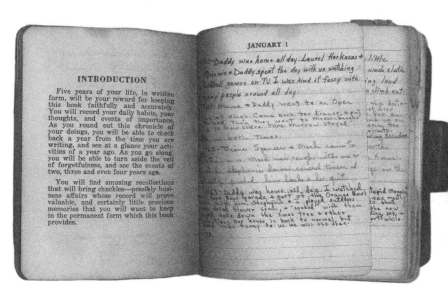

today," or a snowstorm. I'd describe a little bit about it. Many years later, I was able to take those calendars and write almanacs for *Big River* magazine. I had a monthly column that was called the

River Almanac, which was a chronology of the goings-on along the river for that month. I did sixty months, five years' worth of those. They were incorporated in my first book, condensed down considerably. However, the point is to recall, record—then it's more meaningful.

You can do that in the backyard, out on a field trip, hiking, canoeing, cross-country skiing, snowshoeing. There is always time to record what's going on around you. I highly recommend journaling. Photos, having a little camera…nowadays cameras are even on telephones, the way they tell me. So, you can record an awful lot that way—one snap of the camera. Any way you do it is fine.

The Book of Tracks

The wild things in the natural world write a book of their own, especially in the wintertime; that book is *The Book of Tracks*. Wherever they go, wild things leave a sign of their passing. It is a great passing parade of wild critters, birds. You can tell much by simply following a critter track and seeing where it slept last night. Was it a rabbit? Did it go in a brush pile? Oh, I see—a red fox track has joined the rabbit. So now you are following a drama between the red fox and the rabbit. You see where the red fox finds the rabbit in the brush pile. Maybe there are widespread leaps of the rabbit where it runs for its life. Maybe there will be some fur there and a little bit of blood, and you know that the fox went to bed with a full belly.

One can tell a lot about who's living in the place where you are walking, simply by reading that book of tracks. And you can register that in your journal—you didn't see the critters, but you saw their story, you read their story. There are two squirrels, three rabbits, an owl; there's some other birds that left tracks, and there's a whitetail deer track; if you are fortunate, you may see a coyote track. So, once you start to interpret tracks and know what you are looking at, *The Book of Tracks* becomes easy reading. Maybe you will see, on a warm winter evening, the prints of a raccoon or an opossum. They don't hibernate; they just go into a deep sleep. On a warm evening in midwinter,

Exploring the Natural World 37

they will come out of their hollow tree or their den in the rocks, and they will move about. So, it's like any other reading that one does—it should be done thoroughly, and it will bring you a lot of joy and knowledge. Even though you may not see a solitary critter in person, *The Book of Tracks* is required reading.

Respecting Nature

"That's really cool," says the girl. "Sometimes the boys make fun of me because I like to read books. But I bet they don't know about *The Book of Tracks!*"

"And maybe that's something you can tell them about," the river rat says. "Every time we share what we love about nature, the circle widens. We shouldn't keep the miracles to ourselves, but rather we should encourage everyone to participate. That can be hard when people tease you..."

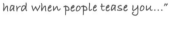

To become an explorer, one needs a certain amount of curiosity and, at times, a certain amount of courage. This courage comes in many ways, one of them being, perhaps, doing something a little different than your classmates or your brothers and sisters. Maybe they don't like snakes. Maybe they don't like to go outside—but that doesn't mean you can't, that you shouldn't. Try to follow your interests, even reading. Books are incredibly important because you can take that book on the rainiest of days, the nastiest days, and you can curl up in the house, and the book will take you somewhere. It's wonderful—reading is incredible. It's a beautiful thing that we are able to read and understand. Don't worry about what others say.

To be an explorer in the natural world is a very natural thing. All of us came from hunter-gathers, regardless of one's ancestry. Somehow, when we became so-called civilized and settled down in certain areas, we began to lose a little of that. These days, we don't use our nose a whole lot; I like to say we don't smell good. Our sense of hearing is not the greatest. We are mostly visually oriented now, especially with our computers and movies and television. There are ways to sharpen those senses when one is exploring. The main thing is not to hurry. Life's too short to hurry through it. There is no need to rush. The slower one goes, the more one listens, smells, and touches things, the better the experience of exploring.

I would certainly say that I am a slow talker, a slow walker, a slow driver. My totem, as I mentioned, is the turtle, and I have much in common with turtles. The turtle was the first mobile home ever made. The turtle says, "This is a good place to be." It might be in the middle of the highway, which isn't a great place to be, however. But they just stop where they feel like stopping, and they're at home. That is what I always try to imitate as much as I can; don't let myself get rushed.

Exploring the natural world is so exciting because you never know what you are going to find. It is true exploration. You might have an idea of what will happen or what you are going to see or smell or taste or touch or hear; however, it usually ends up a little different than what you figured, and usually for the better. It's something you have no clue was going to happen. All we need to do is to tuck those experiences and adventures away for another day, and we bring them out again and think them over again, relive them.

Computers are not the only things in our lives that can store information; our own brains are pretty darn good at that, although I once talked to a fellow who said he knew so much he has to forget something in order to learn something new—that his brain was full.

I would like to know something about everything rather than everything about something, and that you can do when you explore the natural world. There are those people who are entomologists (people who know everything about insects), let's say, but, on the other hand, don't know much about mammals or birds. I think that one is fortunate if one doesn't know everything about one thing.

Building a Fire

Another essential thing to know for exploring and being in nature is how to build a good fire. Most people tend to build huge fires—this is a mistake. When you have a huge fire in the cold, you end up roasting on one side and freezing on the other, turning yourself like a hog on a spit. With a small fire, you can get up close. And it saves a lot on fuel. I tend to build a small fire circle, just for that reason, and, of course, once you get the rocks heated, you get warm from them as well.

A campfire is mesmerizing. You sit a few people down by a campfire, it isn't long before they aren't talking so much—they are looking, watching those flames. Something about that is embedded in our nature from way, way back, when fires were an absolute necessity. A fire is a living thing, even though it comes from dead wood. The fire talks to you; you can hear the sparks snapping and jumping. At night, some sparks fly up to join the stars— I don't think they ever get there. The fire shows you many different colors: burgundy, yellows, oranges, greens, blue. Even the waste of a fire, the ashes, can be used on the land to make the soil more productive, the same way animal waste is used.

So you see, a fire draws everybody closer together, which is, I think, a good thing. That in itself does wonders for people's relationships. A group of people who never met each other in their whole life, total strangers, sit down around a campfire and within an hour or two they are no longer strangers. They will talk and open up, they will remember each other. In the right place, used in the right way, fire is quite wonderful!

To make my fire, I always use wood shavings. I also soak corncobs in kerosene. That's your torch—kerosene is what burns. Kerosene is not like gasoline; it won't go *poof*. A few days to soak, and it will burn quite a while. Then you need your flint and steel or a lighter or matches—modern technology, huh?

It's a wonderful old skill, to know how to start a fire. If you fall through the ice or get caught in the cold and you need to make a fire *now*, you need to be equipped. So, I always carry a couple of cobs and some kindling and can make a fire, even on a rainy or snowy day.

Respecting Nature

Falling through the ice is a bad one when you are by yourself. When I am out on the ice, I always carry a little hand axe in my hind pocket. I had big pockets, so I could reach in there and get that axe in a jiffy. Why is that important? If you fall through the ice, you have no grip—everything around you is slippery, you can't get purchase to get out. You have one good chance to reach the axe out as far as you can and hit the ice hard with the blade and hope it holds. When you pull yourself out of the hole, lie flat on the ice and crawl away. Less chance of breaking the ice again. If you lose your axe, you can't grip, and everything is just numb and you get tired.

I once tipped a canoe over on shelf ice. I was standing there in the water about belly deep, holding onto the canoe, foolishly. I should have let it go, but I didn't know where it would end up. I was in an open channel with ice on each side, which is called shelf ice. The canoe was about half full of water, so I took a trapping glove and tried to bail the canoe out with that trapping glove.

Then I said to myself, "You know, I'm getting tired; I think I'm going to lie down a while." I had hypothermia right then: irrational thinking. I thought, *Oh, no.* I said, "Good-bye, canoe," and I shoved that thing out of there and got myself out of the water. By the time I got back to the tent camp, I was mighty close to dropping over. There is nobody to help you if you are by yourself. So you always have to be prepared when you are exploring, and always remember that you are in the wild, that you have to respect the wild.

Creatures
Tame and Wild

"Gee, you sure know a lot about being outside," the boy says, wide-eyed. "On the way here, Mom said something about river rats being too stubborn to freeze to death, too full of hot air to drown, and too independent to call anyone boss. Now I get what she means!"

Laughter fills the early evening sky, and a hearty pop sounds from the campfire.

The girl looks at the river rat with concern. "Were you really all by yourself out here? That's scary, isn't it? Didn't you ever get lonely?..."

Oh sure, I got lonely out here sometimes. However, when you have a dog, that helps. Also, I have a lot of wild friends. I had a pair of squirrels named Dusky and Red who lived out here in that tree that ended up as the outhouse (it was hollow). Dusky was a black squirrel and Red was a fox squirrel. I took corncobs, and every day I would shell corn off, and they would come down the tree and take it from my hand. This made me smile. Their little whiskers and cold noses would tickle my hand and I would say, "Do you think it's going to snow tomorrow, Dusky? How did you sleep last night, Red? The red-tailed hawk has been around—don't be lying on those branches sunning yourselves."

They say it's okay to talk to things like that, as long as you don't answer. I did some answering as well, from time to time. There was a pair of geese named Big Boy and Beauty who lived right out here on Big Lake. I had a dock down here back then, and I could go out to visit with them. I would say, "Beauty, your little goslings are so pretty this year." Seven fluffy yellow little balls floating on the water. I could watch them grow.

I take a lot of pleasure in mice—there are still plenty of them around the shack. They run on the edge of these flat-plate rafters, all the way around. When you are in bed at night, and you have a kerosene lamp flickering, or the fire, you watch them play. I always took a lot of pleasure watching mice and bats. Bats, at night, would come in and out. I used to have an old screen door, so I could let them in and out.

Fall was always a melancholy time, when ducks and geese, songbirds and swans were migrating south. They were leaving me, and I longed already for spring, when they would come back again. A solitary life is gratifying on one hand and frustrating on the other—it's very taxing on one, especially physically. You roast in the summer, you freeze in the winter.

One can learn an awful lot from watching the critters and birds. What is their life all about?

Next time it's twenty below zero and the wind is blowing, and you are snuggled up in your nice warm bed in your nice warm house with a full belly, think about the wild things: where are they tonight? Some hibernate; they say, "Heck with it all," and go to sleep for a few months. But a lot of them have to eat something every day. The chickadee is my favorite bird, because they are so tiny and cheerful. I love their personality—the chickadee is happy and bouncing around; however, they have to eat their weight in seeds every day just to survive.

Imagine sitting in a tree someplace, even in a coniferous tree, all night long in the winter, twelve hours or more of nighttime and that wind blowing. It ain't no Sunday school picnic—it's tough. So, there again, one can help those critters and feed them some seeds or whatever they are eating. I don't care if the squirrels come to my bird feeders and eat the birdseed. They got to live too, and it isn't an easy life. Sometimes feeding them is not helping them—like with bears. "A fed bear is a dead bear" is the old saying because bears who get used to being fed are going to get into trouble. Using the knowledge we get from exploring the natural world, in a respectful way, is what we need to do: help critters. Critters need homes and grocery stores; we call it *habitat*. That's why Aldo Leopold talked often about the land ethic, that the land should not be looked at as a commodity to be bought and sold for a profit. It has to be looked at with the idea that we are a part of that land. It's not ours; it belongs to those who have been here before us and those who come after. I believe exploring the natural world will teach a person that.

Squirrels are wonderful to examine too, because the squirrels and chipmunks have a layaway plan. They have learned long ago that one must save up for winter; even though they are probably only a couple months old, these little critters know, naturally, they must store, they must save—that's a valuable lesson.

I once saw a water snake with a great big frog in its mouth. The snake was going to eat it. It had ahold of the frog by the hind legs. The snake wasn't real big. The frog was a good-sized leopard frog. The poor thing was crying out, I guess you could say. I rarely interfere with that cycle, but let's face it: in the circle, one thing eats another, and it's not always pretty, and it's not always easy to stand by. Well, I interfered and I took that frog away from the snake. It wasn't easy; I got its mouth pried open. I don't know, maybe the frog didn't even live. It was just one of those things.

It's nice to hear the blackbirds. They are harbingers of autumn. There are lots of blackbirds, a wonderful thing to watch. They roost in bottomland, then in the morning they fly out to the cornfields. If you ever watch them, the whole flock undulates up and down like a roller coaster. They all go up and swoop around in unison.

Farmers aren't real fond of blackbirds, but hey, that's the way it is. They have these little gas-carbine guns that simulate a gunshot, set on a timer. Every so often you hear a pop when it goes off. It works for a while, then the birds figure it out, thinking, *Uh, nothing happens to us; not a one of us that came back to roost was wounded tonight. I don't think those things are real...I think we are going to eat here.* Geese are also famous for that;

on golf courses where people don't want the birds they call it hazing the geese, but that doesn't work forever, either.

Corvids are some of the most intelligent birds on earth—crows, ravens, blue jays. They have their own language they are talking, but I don't know what they are saying exactly. All things in the natural world talk, not like they do in Disney movies, perhaps, but they do communicate through body language and chemically, and they communicate with their voices in a great many ways. But we don't know what they are saying half of the time. We have not learned all of that.

Work Lessons

One of the funniest things I ever saw was a group of baby river otters. I was paddling a canoe, and the mother otter swam up alongside me. She had three little babies—well, they were about the size

of a mink. They kind of chitter and chirp in the
water. I pulled over against the bank and watched
them. They went up on the bank and made a slide
out of mud into the water. The mother did all the
slide work, and she took the first trip down. One
after the other, four otters went, round and round
and up and down. It was like at a playground,

watching little kindergartners on a slide. They had so much fun, I had to laugh, because I had fun too.

The otter is one of the critters that has made play out of its work. Otters are tremendous swimmers and catch fish on the swim. They drag them out on the ice in the wintertime; they have several holes in the ice that they keep open so they can fish. They locate these schools of fish, then they work in that area for a week or two. However, they are big travelers, and they travel a big area, then they come back again. Even when they are working (catching fish), they play a lot and chase each other in the snow and dive into those holes, two, three of them, and chase each other around—under the ice, I imagine. They have learned how to make their work into enjoyment, into play. There aren't many critters that have done that, even us—we people sure have a hard time doing that. So, if you can get paid to do something that you really enjoy doing, that's it right there. That's the ultimate.

Of Snakes and Bees, and Good and Bad

It was the spring of the year. I was traveling by canoe and had my dog in the front of the canoe, as usual. Her name was Joey, she was a female black lab, and she was getting up in the years. It was that time of year when the ice had just melted and the wood ducks were coming back. They were sitting on the logs preening each other and talking back and forth. The wild geese were flying north to nest, the red-winged blackbirds were sitting on the cattails singing their springtime song.

For the first time, the sun felt good on one's cheek and the wind blew from the south. Along about noon we came to the old tent camp area, and my eyes were heavy; I wanted to take a nap.

So I pulled in by the old tent camp, and I took a walking stick along with me and went up the old wooden steps. I knew I would have company in my tent camp, because the water was a little bit high, and there was no door on the tent, only a canvas flap. Now, I never minded sharing my shacks with critters—after all I was living in their homes. However, I was not crazy about the idea of sleeping with them. So I walked over to the army cot, took the walking stick, and used it to pick up the pillow—there was a big fat water snake sleeping!

Well, now I had three choices: use my walking stick right there and kill that snake, throw it outside, and the owls and the mink would eat it up, and I would never have to deal with that critter again. However, I killed many critters so that I might live myself, but I never kill one to watch the fire of life go out of its eyes—that's not a valid reason to kill anything. I had a second choice: to go to a different shack. But I'm standing right here by the army cot, so I opted for the third choice. I reached under that snake with the walking stick, picked him up, and carried him over and put

him in the corner. He was rolling now, so I took
a gunnysack, a burlap bag, put it on top of him,
put the stick on top of the bag, and let him mel-
low out a little bit. Well, he settled down. I reckon
he thought to himself, *Well, it isn't so bad here. It's
dark, I feel fairly safe, I might be able to catch a frog
or a mouse for supper.*

Then I crawled up on that old army cot and
my old dog crawled up right alongside me, stretch-
ing out there. I was just about to check out the
inside of my eyelids when I look up at the ceiling
and see there is a hole in the canvas. Can't have
that, because by fall everything in that place will
be rotten. So I make a mental note to go back
there in the summertime to patch that hole. So on
a hot day in July, I load the old dog in the canoe,
I take some tar and some canvas, and I make my
way down to the tent camp. I get there and walk
inside. I look up at the ceiling, down at the floor,
and I see that I'm too short on one end—I can't
reach that hole and patch it. I get to looking further around that camp. I see there is a five-gallon
pail tipped upside down over a stump; it's been
there all summer long.

A light bulb comes on—I thought, *I can go down there, get that pail, put it upside down, stand on it, and reach that hole and patch it.* So, I start down the old wooden steps, the old dog with me, step by step, just like a shadow. I go over by that pail, and I no more than touch it, wiggle it a little bit, and the biggest swarm of bees you ever see in your life comes out from under there. They cover me, they cover the old dog, they get to stinging. Now there is only one thing you can do about that time: run just as fast as you can! Well, maybe there are two things you could do—you can run and you can scream at the same time.

I focused more on the running…thought that would be more productive. I headed for the nearest Mississippi slough to jump into, get some relief from them bees. Well, the old dog was old but she could run faster than me—she passes me, jumps into the slough, leaves me with the bees. I'm picking them up and laying them down as fast as I can. Did you ever hear of Bo Jackson, who was considered the fastest human being on earth? I could have beat Bo Jackson in a hundred-yard dash about that time. Got to the edge of that slough. Now, the Mississippi slough in the summer-time is covered with green duckweed. Duckweed is the smallest flowering plant in the world; every single one of those specks is a plant unto itself.

Under the duckweed is some water, in the water are some fish and frogs, turtles and snakes, and under the water is that black, boot-sucking Mississippi mud. Black, boot-sucking Mississippi mud is that stuff when you are walking through it with rubber boots on, you get a funny feeling in one foot and you turn around, and there in back of you is one of your boots, sticking in the mud, sucked right off your foot. That slough looked like a little bit of heaven to me! I laid right flat out and made a water entry that would make any Labrador retriever real proud.

The water sprayed and the mud flew. Then the second worst thing happened to me: I found out the water was too shallow, wouldn't cover me. I had to lay down and roll in the mud—and my blood and the bees. When they were done with me, I had to hold one eye open so that I could see to get me out of the swamp. All swelled up.

Now, I'm very ashamed that I was a poor

student; however, if you would ask me if bees are bad or good I could have spelled you the answer: B-A-D. Nothing good about a bee. But then I got to thinking. Bees pollinate flowers, bees make honey...these bees were only protecting their home. So, I decided that bees were both bad and good at the same time. Isn't that true of all things in the great circle of life? Isn't that true of each and every one of us here?

There's an old saying: There's a little bit of bad in the best of us, and there is a little bit of good in the worst. Alex Haley, the author of *Roots*, every letter he ever wrote to anybody he signed with these words: "Seek the good and praise it." Very wise man, he was. If we look long enough, we will find good in almost any situation, a little bit of good somewhere. However, that is not enough. When we find the good, we need to praise it and say something about it. So often I think we fail there. We might tell somebody else and say, "Oh, didn't Jack do a great job?" But to say it to the person themselves and praise them—that is what counts.

Dogs
I Have Known

The kids and their parents laugh at the image of the muddy river rat and his dog in the swamp.

"We have a dog too," says the girl. "His name is Rascal. Sometimes Dad gets annoyed when he digs big holes in the backyard. But he sleeps with me really nice and can do neat tricks, like rolling over—I guess that's what you mean by praising the good, huh?"

The river rat smiles and nods.

"What's your dog's name?" asks the boy. "And how long have you had her?..."

I have always kept a dog, sometimes two, with me out here. They are good company and good workers as well.

Their noses would have scars from fighting with critters, and they would always want to catch a critter for old Dad. They always had to know which way the shack was; blinding snowstorms, pea-soup fog—I just couldn't be watching them all the time. They had to learn how to walk on thin ice. Once they knew about ice, they had so much better feeling for the ice than I did, so I would follow them across the ice. They also needed to learn how to ride in a canoe.

When I got a new dog, I put him in the front of a canoe. I would say sit, stay. You know how young dogs are—there was no way they were going to sit and stay very long. I didn't want to be tipped over in the black, boot-sucking Mississippi mud. So I would go over to the bank and cut me a willow whip, long and slender with a whippy tip; not going to hurt them, but I can reach up and touch them meaningfully, when need be. I put that willow whip in the canoe and set off down through the sloughs. It wasn't too long when that young dog was looking up at the birds, leaning over the side, lapping at the water, sniffing every branch or twig that came by, jumping back and forth. I picked up that willow whip and I would whop her once, twice, three times; I would say sit, stay! After about three ten-hour days, that young dog was trained to ride in a canoe. She enjoyed the ride and so did I.

When I got out on the bank, my dog ran to me, licked my face, wagged her tail, and she said, *I don't care what you did to me, Pa, the last few days. I love you anyway.* That is called unconditional love. Therein lies the difference between human character and critter character: in general, a critter character is much more forgiving and loving than human character.

Spider and Webster

I had all different kinds of dogs. Most were some sort of water breed, like a Lab, Chesapeake, or a golden retriever; many of them were mixed breeds. Last year, I lost the last one that really was out here with me full time. He was fourteen and a half, a German shorthair and some kind of hound. He had very short hair, of course, but he thought he was a Labrador retriever. His name was Webster. When I first got Webster, he came to us as a stray and he was full of welts and scars—somebody had just been real nasty to him. He was not full grown and you could count every rib. I had an old Lab at the time named Spider. I thought, *Ah, I'll take Webster along duck hunting*, and I did. He loved to go, but he would never get a

duck; he could swim and all, but he didn't like the idea of pickin' up a duck.

So he was the cheerleader. Spider would go out and get the duck while Webster would jump up and down on the bank like he was saying, "Good girl, Spider! That's the way! Bring 'em in!" One day, Spider was getting arthritic in the joints and quite old. I shot a duck down, and Spider went down to the edge of the water and stopped, turned around, and looked at me as if to say, "No more. It's too cold. I'm not doing this no more." On Webster went, right by her, jumped into the water, swam out, got the duck, brought it back. From that day he said, "I can do that." He was not equipped to do that; however, he did the duck hunting every day that I went. It was another lesson that nature had taught: if you think you can do something, in all probability you will be able to. You learn so much from dogs.

Old Spook

My first dog, the oldest, Old Spook, lived to be sixteen. One day years ago, we went out and sat by a swamp white oak and remembered old times. He died within a few days; whenever I get a new swamp dog, I go there with him. It's a place known only to me. We go there and I remember the lessons I learned from that old dog. First thing he taught me about: time. That in banking terms, yesterday is a canceled check, tomorrow is a promissory note, today is ready cash.

During those years in the swamp, I took up a most peculiar hobby called reading. I was a very poor reader, a very poor student. However, I would have the kerosene lamps going, and I would play catch-up. I don't mean the kind you put on your hamburgers. Catch-up is played this way: you get a book, you read, and when you come across a word you don't know, you take down another book, called *Webster's Dictionary*, you look up that word, then you learn to pronounce it and how to spell it and use it in its correct context. I played a lot of catch-up, and I once read a quote, "It's better to have loved someone or something and lost it than to have never loved anyone or anything at all." My second lesson. The old dog had opened and softened my heart.

The third thing he taught me about was the great circle of life: that life and death are one and the same, there is no difference between the two. We generally do not ask to be born, and we generally do not ask to die. We all must do them, both things. Without new life there would be no death, and without death there would be no new life. It's a paradox; that's the way it works. So, there again I learned a lot about the natural world from my dog.

Mango

I got my latest dog, Mango, a female black Lab, at a no-kill shelter—she had been in there five months. The people at the rescue shelter said, "Well, take her for a walk." There is about an acre of land there. Well, she took *me* for the walk…just about yanked my arm from the sockets! And she is still that way on a leash. She hates to be penned up. I knew why she was in the shelter for so long—whoever took her for a walk got a good going-over. I thought, *Ah, she reminds me of my old Joey.* I said, "Let's take her anyhow," and we did.

Thirty dollars is all they wanted, and she had been spayed and had all of her shots. We thought that was awful cheap, and so we gave them a hundred bucks; they do good work, and we gave them another hundred at Christmastime.

We took Mango home about a year ago. At first, she was "trouble"; she would run away on us. She just wanted to run, leave her out of that house. I mean she was just like a black shot, just gone, and she would not stop. We have eighty acres of land, and she might be gone for, goodness, an hour, and we would worry about her. We carried these little doggy bones, we'd call her, and, little by little, she'd come and we would give her one of them. I guess she kind of thought, *Hey, that's not a bad thing when I come.* She's getting a lot better now.

She can swim forever. She couldn't swim at first (never been in the water, I guess), but after a few days she got it. Now she will swim after a teaching dummy until I can't throw the thing anymore. Riding in a canoe…well, she still has a little to learn there, but it will come. She is an awful good pal.

Dogs have a glaring defect: they don't live long enough. It takes you three, four years just to get really bonded, then you got maybe another five years of goodness; by the time they are ten, they are starting to go downhill. But they are wonderful.

People would come here to do an interview—for radio, television, or newspaper—and they would always ask me, "If you had one thing you could change about your life, what would it be?" I would invariably say, "I would want to be more like a dog." It's true. They give unconditional love. They don't care how you look or how you smell, they don't care about what station in life you have—don't mean nothing. They take you for you, and they give you everything they can. They ask for little in return: a pat on the head, something to eat, place to sleep. That's it. Don't have to be fancy.

Hunting, Trapping, and Fishing

"We sure love Rascal," the girl says, sharing a smile with her mom.

"Maybe we could take Rascal hunting..." the boy adds, thinking. "You said before that the only skills you had were fishing and trapping," he continues. "What animals do you trap, and are you good at it? Dad says he'll teach me if I want."

"He said he'd teach both of us," the girl corrects. "I like the fish Dad brings home from his fishing trips...but it makes me sad to think of animals suffering. I mean, I know we need to eat, but there has to be a good way to do it, right?"

When you go out fishing, hunting, or trapping, it is not about catching or getting an animal; these things give you an *opportunity* to catch something—maybe you will, maybe you won't. It's an exploration. That's what it's about. It's about sitting in that canoe or that boat and seeing the great blue heron and listening to its raucous call and watching a real angler fish, patience galore, wading slowly. That critter has to catch something. It's not a matter of whether they want to or not—that is real catching right there.

I don't trap any land animals. I used to. I simply just don't have the heart for it anymore, so I don't do it. For water animals, I use a conibear trap. This is a kill trap, the first of its kind, and it is still just as good as any other trap ever invented. Any trap has to be set with the thought of being as humane as possible. Think of the animal first; think of catching the animal for its fur, for yourself, second—because no animal deserves to be maimed or tortured in any way. The same thing if you're hunting. What I would consider a good hunter is one who will pass up an opportunity to shoot at something if he's not sure he's going to kill

Hunting, Trapping, and Fishing

that animal quickly. Wounding it can happen, but it's not a good thing.

I was a muskrat trapper, for the most part. That's what lives here. The muskrat season runs from mid-November until the first of March. There is no limit to how many you catch—not legally there isn't. However, whether we are fishing, hunting, or trapping, there is *always* a limit. The limit is what the population can bear, in good stead. To fill one's game bag, or an ice cooler when you are fishing, just to say, "I got the limit!"—no, that's not a good thing, that isn't how it works. There are no ethics involved then.

There are legal laws and there are what are called moral or ethical laws. The ethical laws are not printed in regulations when you buy a license. I think it wouldn't be a bad idea, but I guess you can't legislate morality. You can suggest and perhaps through role modeling do more than any other way. It just doesn't work to stand up before a podium, pound your fist on the podium, and give a rousing speech—people don't like to be preached to, so I think suggestion and role modeling is a good way to teach morals.

When I set traps, I always make sure to have the right tools. I have rubber gloves that reach up to your shoulder and are insulated, which is nice for an old man. The water feels colder every year. Since you are placing the trap in the water, it is important to keep your arms warm and dry. I also use willow stakes to mark where the traps are. I peel them for two reasons: first thing is not to feed the beaver, or the stakes will be gone in the morning and you don't know where your trap is. The second reason is for longevity: they last longer when they are peeled. A willow stake like this will last at least five years' daily use.

Once again, walking sticks—they test the depth of the water, what's under there, logs or mud. You can find muskrat runs; when there is no ice, you will feel where they are with the stick. There is just no end to the use of a walking stick.

Once the animal is caught, you have to dry it. You never skin a wet animal. After skinning, you flesh and stretch them (in other words, scrape the fat and meat off), turn them inside out to do that, and then put them on a stretcher and dry them completely, which takes about a week. Then they are ready for sale. I believe in taking care of your own furs—nowadays the fur buyers will buy them just the way they come out of the water. I think it might be just a little bit disrespectful, throwing 'em down on the floor and saying, here. It's a good skill, an ancient skill, to care for furs properly. It gives you another advantage if you go to the fur buyer with green muskrats (that means "just-skinned"). If they're not stretched and dried, you don't have many choices. If you take them dried properly and don't like the price that is being offered, you can pack them back up in your cardboard box and go home. So you have an advantage in that respect.

Muskrat for Supper

Of course, the fur is only part of the animal, and out of respect for nature you have to use as much of the animal as you can. Squirrels, if cooked properly, are good. But one time I ate one that was probably old enough to vote...something was different. But I was hungry. I shot this great big red fox squirrel, and when I skinned it, it was tough, almost hidebound. I cooked that thing and parboiled it and then roasted it—it was still like shoe leather. I could have fed it to my dog, I guess, but I even hated to do that. However, the dog did get about half of that squirrel. It was just not edible. That was probably the worst thing I have ever eaten.

Muskrat, I would say, is comparable to duck. It's all dark meat like a duck, a lot of the same taste. You only use the hind—it's called a muskrat saddle. It's cut off at the pelvis where you've got the two legs, the back end. There is very little on the front legs and the ribs. Muskrats are not that big; a big one weighs two and a half pounds. The best thing I have eaten out here, though, is the mud cat, a flathead catfish. The cheeks from the catfish are just delicious. They are not the prettiest fish in the world. Walleyes are good, but mud cat will beat them every time.

Lessons from Nature

"I guess times are kinda different now, huh?" the boy asks, looking for answers in the adults' faces.

"Yes and no," his mom says slowly. "There have been some good things about what we call progress, some inventions that help us in a good way; but there are also some things I could do without...And as far as nature and the wilderness—well, they still exist, though we're making them smaller. But lots of us still have our love of nature. Many of us still feel the pull to be outdoors, discovering the hundreds of daily miracles that are happening right in front of us. And many of us still want to share that with others," she says, smiling at the group. "So some things remain the same."

"What do you think?" the boy asks the river rat. "You're older than my parents. How have you seen stuff change?"

We have been studying the natural world for thousands of years, but we are still finding out a lot of new things. One of them, just in perhaps the past half century, is that everything in the natural circle of life needs each other and is interconnected. If one thing is gone, it will be sorely missed by all the rest. That is a great question answered.

The two great resources in this world are natural resources and human resources—that is all we have. As the natural resources go, so will the human resources. That, sad to say, was found out by a great many ancient cultures. Even Native Americans, who, I would say, have the greatest respect overall for the circle of life, were not without some failures. There is a place called Cahokia down toward Saint Louis that was thought to be the largest Native American city ever. Probably 30,000 to 40,000 people lived there, and their demise was caused by denuding a 200-mile radius around the city: no trees, no wood left to heat or to

cook with. So, I guess we must learn from our past. That way we can decide what to do today and where we are going in the future.

Be Different

Konrad Lorenz was a famous animal behaviorist, one of the pioneers along the Rhine River after World War II. He studied ravens and other corvids. They would literally go on walks with him—they would follow him, fly as he walked. He kept them in his house, and he learned a lot about the language of corvids, because he dared to be different. It isn't bad to be different. There is a lot of pressure, of course, to not be different.

I guess that is one reason why I lived the way I did. I never felt like I fit in with the so-called normal society. However, now the "normal" folks, quite a number of them, are taking up my abnormal ways. Wildlife viewing is one of the fastest growing recreational activities in the world—incredible! It is nonconsumptive, and it is there for the next person. There is a federal program called Watchable Wildlife, and each state has its own guide to wildlife. They tell you where you can see various critters, how to get to those places, what time of the year is best for different critters, and stuff like that. So, I think we are on the right path with this Watchable Wildlife. So-called silent sports—kayaking, canoeing, hiking, birding—are going to be one of the answers.

A Changing World

The old-timers that I knew had one of the most horrible diets you could ever imagine. They ate lard a lot. Lard is the fat of the pig that is rendered.

Rendering is the process of boiling it down, then you let it cool, and you have a white salvelike material called lard. The old-timers would take homemade bread and smear lard on there and salt it for a sandwich—it's a dietitian's nightmare. They ate a lot of smoked meats and lots of taters. Three meals a day they would eat potatoes...all bad things, we are told, and yet, my grandmother on my mother's side lived to be almost ninety-nine, my grandfather eighty-eight, my grandmother on my father's side eighty-nine, and my other grandfather was eighty—he died youngest of the four.

However, I think part of the reason they lived so long was that they did a lot of physical work. Even in their everyday life, they had to pump water each day from a hand pump and carry it inside, get firewood in and make a fire for not only heating but for cooking, and they washed their clothes on a washboard or by hand. Their everyday life was so much more physical than ours is today—we go turn the tap on for water, we turn the thermostat on and we get heat. So what do we do? We run up and down the roads or walk on treadmills. Stores are built on one level, basically;

it's the new style, what they call big box stores. Why not build them about seven stories high and have people walk up those steps to do their shopping? They might not have to run up and down the road then. Folks unable to use steps would have to use an elevator. I'm not finding fault, necessarily; I'm just reporting it like it basically is.

Our lifestyle today does not seem to invite us to go exploring the great circle of life and the natural world. We are getting further and further removed from that. Automobiles everywhere, highways, places we could just as well (in a lot of cases) walk or bicycle to—but we've come to rely on the automobile. All those highways and parking lots are places where the rain can't soak in. It runs off and that's called "development."

So, we develop more and more of our land, not only to live on but to support us in the forms of stores and highways and transportation. But we do have to remember that agricultural land is what feeds us, for the most part, and we've got to have that—we've got to have as much of that as possible. Loss of our agricultural land is a very worrisome thing.

When we explore the natural world, we simply *must* remember to set aside green places, wild places. When we get to know and love and respect the wild things, we will want to protect and preserve the wild places, so to begin exploring at an early age is critical. It's absolutely crucial that happens.

A lot of us grew up interacting with the natural world. I grew up in the hill country, close to

the Mississippi River, third longest river in the world. It's a world resource. It was always available to me, and there was no fear of bad things out there. Mother would say, even in the wintertime when the temperature was well below zero, "You get your clothes on, dress up warm, and get out of the house now. Carry in some wood, do something. But be back for supper." So that was a whole different ball game. Now, of course, we have fewer and fewer places to go out and explore. We simply must have them—we have to keep those places. We can't keep them all, I know that, because we are getting more and more people. But we need to keep some wild places.

Will Rogers once said, "Land is one thing they ain't making no more of." If it was true then, what is it today when you have a population that is hundreds of times bigger than back then? It's simply a matter of getting out there and learning about the wild things, and the rest will fall into place.

The whole idea of land ownership somehow never struck me quite right. We do not own our houses or our metal cocoons that we run up and down the road in; we don't own our bank accounts, we certainly can't own the land, we cannot own the moonbeams, the rays of sun, the snowflakes, raindrops that fall upon the earth, nor the wind that blows across it.

When we purchase land, we purchase a privilege—a privilege of being a good steward of that land—then we turn it over to someone else along with everything else I just mentioned. However, we do own our time. None of us knows how much of it we have. We are standing somewhere and someone says, "What are you doing today, Joe?" You say, "Oh, just killing time." That is a bad thing to kill. If you want to kill time, go out exploring the natural world and spend it there. Time will become more precious and more meaningful.

Revolution or Education

There are only two ways to change the world: revolution and education. You would think the sensible person would choose the latter, education. However, there is a problem with education. It takes a long time to see any results. It's like casting seeds; you cast the seeds, some fall on fertile ground, and in a year or two you see a beautiful flower, while some fall on fallow ground and twenty, thirty years they lay there...but eventually they will grow. We *must* cast the seeds or nothing will grow.

Yet, education is one of the first things on the chopping block when the budgets are figured out. However, education will never cost as much as ignorance. We should rethink that idea, and we will. The young folks are the great hope—there is no other hope. Just look at recycling; it took us forever to figure out we can use something more than once. Nowadays, every schoolchild knows about recycling: put that piece in that bin, and you put this piece over there, and it's all reused. We have Adopt a Highway now, and we pick up after ourselves for a change (We have that on the river as well: the Adopt an Island program). Littering has become a lot less of a problem. If you go down the road and take a candy bar out, unwrap it, crinkle the paper up, roll the window down, a little voice in the backseat will say, "Don't do that. That's littering and that's not good." The proof is in the pudding. Our attitudes and values are changing and that's good.

I always thought that nature is a common denominator. If the president comes here and he and I take a canoe out and a big dark cloud comes rolling over the Minnesota bluffs and it starts to pour, he's going to get just as wet as I am. I once did some school projects where school board members, principals, superintendents, teachers, and I would all go afield (we did this during each of the four seasons). By the end of the very first day, they were calling each other by their first names—it wasn't *Mr.* or *Mrs.* Smith. Everyone was dirty and tired and hungry. Nature will do that. Station in life don't mean nothing.

Maybe we could have a bunch of fire circles constructed in Washington, DC. We'd have two from each party at each fire. These folks might get to know and understand each other. I wouldn't doubt it might work.

Share Nature and Teach Others

Some of us had mentors—a grandfather, a father, an older brother, maybe an uncle—somebody who went exploring and said, "You want to go along?"

Maybe it was fishing, hiking, just watching the geese, or other simple things. "Do you want to make a walking stick?" We were very fortunate, those of us who had a mentor. That's not necessarily the case anymore. A lot of people don't have that opportunity to have a mentor. That's why it's so crucial for women, in particular, to be involved in exploring the natural world. Because in most families, it's usually the woman, the mother, who will raise the children, with some help, but it's mostly her influence, and if she does not love and respect the natural world, neither will the children. Generally, Mom is the most influential.

So, it is very important for girls of every age to learn about nature. I think sometimes we shun them, almost. As though girls are not able or not supposed to do certain outdoor activities—but of course they are! We men need to change our attitudes and values. I do see some improvement there, like hunter safety courses and such: there are a lot more girls now than used to be involved in that class. You don't have to go hunting just because you take a hunter safety course. It teaches one to respect and use a firearm safely. You don't

have to go hunting at all. Hunting is not about
killing to begin with. It gives one an opportunity
to kill something, perhaps, but you don't have to.
᾿s important to learn these sorts of life skills.
᾿ixty-eight years old, and I'm still

Muskrat for Supper

exploring and finding all kinds of new things. That is one of the beautiful things about it! Playing football, hockey, basketball, any of the so-called sports, will come to an end as one gets older, but exploring the natural world will not. That's a lifelong interest, a lifelong commitment; that's the beautiful part about it. It's just incredible.

A Special Story

"Wow! You're sixty-eight?!" says the boy. "And you still like exploring? Lots of grownups I know don't really like to go on adventures."

"Hey, now. Don't beat up on grownups too much, kiddo," his dad interrupts. "I bet those adults you're talking about used to go on plenty of adventures. Maybe they just can't get around as easily anymore. But I bet they have lots of memories of those days, poking around their woods, heading out on hikes, watching critters, and discovering fresh tracks."

Mom chimes in. "And I bet they tell those memories to their kids and grandkids, and maybe even the kids in their neighborhoods. That's how we all learn to appreciate wild things. Speaking of stories, I'm guessing our friend the river rat has more to tell."

"Sure enough," the river rat says. "You might even recognize the folks in this next one..."

Ellie and Jack sat side by side on the back porch steps. The late October sun felt good as they rested. Piles of leaves dotted the lawn around them, and their rakes were propped against the side of the house. They watched as Lance, who had just turned thirteen last week, held a large plastic bag open while his younger sister, Katie, shoved and scooped the leaf piles into the bag.

Just then a small flock of Canada geese flew overhead, following their ancient pathway in the sky to the south. Jack gazed up, watching the geese across the sky until they were out of sight. Ellie looked over. "You still miss those hunting and trapping years, don't you, Jack?"

He thought a moment, then answered, "Yeah, I guess I do. It's just that the sound of those wild geese, the crispness and smell of autumn air…Well, Ellie, they bring back good memories. And those leaf piles look a little like musk-rat houses in the marsh."

Muskrat for Supper

Ellie smiled and told Jack that he'd always had a vivid imagination. Jack grinned as they both stood, stretched their backs, and picked up the rakes.

Next morning over breakfast, Ellie asked, "When are you going to take it up again, Jack?"

From behind the morning paper Jack murmured, "Take what up?"

"Hunting and trapping," Ellie answered.

Suddenly, it was dead quiet. Spoons fell silent in the cereal bowls. All eyes focused on Jack. He laid the morning paper aside. Ellie broke the silence.

"Katie and Lance, you know your father grew up on the farm and hunted and trapped until he went off to college, right?" They both nodded their heads. Ellie continued, "Well, your father and I met in college. During school vacations, I went along home with your dad and even went hunting and trapping with him quite a few times."

Lance's eyes widened with excitement. "When we gonna go, Dad?!" he blurted out.

"Moooom, hunting and trapping?" Katie challenged. "What's next? Living in a tent and cooking over a campfire? Gross!" and she stuck out her tongue.

Jack looked at Ellie and said, "We'll see about it kids. We'll see."

One evening the week before Thanksgiving, while the family watched TV, Jack made an announcement. "Katie, Lance, your mother and I have decided to spend the weekend with the two of you over on the marsh at Dikesville. The Department of Natural Resources has a little campground there, and the whole marsh is open to hunting and trapping. It's owned by everyone, including us, so let's go see about it, huh?"

Over the next few days, Jack bought his hunting and trapping license, got some trap tags made up, and he and Lance took the old 12-gauge pump shotgun from the closet to be cleaned and oiled. Seven traps were taken down from a nail in the attic, checked over, and tagged with Jack's name and address so everyone would know who was responsible for those traps. The old wood-splitting axe was honed with a file to a razor-sharp edge.

One evening, Ellie and Katie walked into the garage while Jack and Lance were preparing to peel some willow saplings they had cut that afternoon down by the old ditch that ran through the back pasture.

Ellie said, "Katie and I have the camper all cleaned up and ready to go, the food is prepared, the clothes are all packed, and we haven't seen one bit of help from the two of you!" Looking a little frustrated, Ellie continued. "If this is going to be a family adventure, then let's do things that way! Jack, give me that axe. Katie and I are going to peel those trap stakes."

Jack and Lance took turns holding the stakes and loading them into the pickup while Ellie and Katie peeled them.

"Dad, why are we peelin' stakes?" Katie asked.

Jack replied, "Well, Katie, there are two reasons to peel them. First of all, they're willow saplings, which is a soft wood, so they're liable to rot sooner than oak or hickory stakes. Peeling them makes them last longer and also makes for a lighter load to carry. But the main reason has to do with beaver. You see, Katie, willow trees of the small kind are one of the beavers' favorite foods."

Jack paused for a moment. "Actually it's not the tree they're after—it's the bark that they eat. Now, the Dikesville marsh has a mighty healthy population of beavers. If we went there this coming weekend and stuck fresh, unpeeled willows under the ice to hold and mark our traps, we'd just as well be posting a sign saying 'Hey, you beavers, come to each hole in the ice for a free lunch!' We'd be minus a stake, trap, and all when they finished up their lunch." Jack added, "I know it seems like a lot of work now, Katie, but it's worth it in the long run."

A Special Story

Katie nodded. "How'd you ever learn all this stuff, Dad?" she asked.

Jack chuckled. "Why, just by being out there with the critters, I guess, along with listening to the old-timers. And I have to admit that I once stuck a few unpeeled willow stakes in a hole in the ice to hold my traps—and found everything gone in the morning. Maybe that was the best teacher of all."

After the stakes were all peeled and packed away, the four of them checked and rechecked all the gear, then went into the house. While Katie and Lance made microwave popcorn and hot apple cider, Jack and Ellie settled back in their recliners.

Later, just before the lights were turned off for bedtime, Lance said, "Boy, this is cool, ain't it Katie?"

Katie replied, "I guess it isn't as bad as I thought it'd be. We'll see how it goes tomorrow."

In the last flicker of light, Ellie and Jack shared long, slow winks.

The next morning, just after daylight, the foursome unpacked the traps, stakes, lunch, and shotgun at the Dikesville campground. A fresh snowfall of several inches blanketed the frozen ground. The family set off, each with their own gear to carry.

Jack carried the shotgun and a backpack with traps and the axe tied securely to it. Katie was next, her backpack filled with spare clothes and a set of binoculars slung around her neck. Ellie carried a bundle of ten long, slender willows over her shoulder. Bringing up the rear was Lance, small backpack stuffed with sandwiches and a thermos of hot chocolate; in his fanny pack was a set of long rubber trapping gloves.

The family stayed in single file as they walked down the small wooded hillside toward the marsh. Every now and then, Jack would stop to look and listen, pointing out tracks in the fresh snow or identifying bird calls. The family gathered round to read the stories spelled out by the passing parade of wild things as they traveled the ancient circle of life. Reaching the marsh's edge, the family sat down on a fallen log to rest.

As they each helped themselves to a sandwich, they shared half a cup of hot chocolate—and they shared what they'd seen and heard: tracks of fox, squirrel, grouse, and mouse, the wind whipping through the cattails and wild rice stalks, the shrill cry of a red-tailed hawk.

Lance piped up, "Why do we all drink from the same cup, Mom?"

"'Cause when you're in the woods, you don't need all kinds of stuff—it just weighs you down. You share as best you can," Ellie answered.

Katie asked, "Did you hear all the blue jays and crows scolding us?"

"Yep," Ellie offered. "Crows and jays are known as the town criers of the forest. They're very intelligent birds. Anytime they notice intruders, they'll talk about it in a loud way, and all the other creatures will listen and understand that danger has entered the woods."

Lance added, "Don't forget the chickadees." As

he finished his sentence, one landed on a log not far from him. Ellie tossed over a bread crust, and they all watched spellbound as the little bird carried it to a branch above their heads and ate it—a peck at a time—nodding quickly now and then as if to thank them for his meal.

"This log is so old and rotten, bet it won't last much longer, huh, Dad?" Katie wondered.

"Probably not, Katie. All living things are born, they grow and reproduce, then they die and become part of the earth again. In the spring, the green things wake up from the winter's sleep and begin to poke their heads from the ground. They're afraid at first. They say it's still cold up here. However, each day the sun climbs higher, the days grow longer, and the winds turn to the south. Then the warm spring rains begin to fall. The green things begin to gain courage. Soon the grasses stand tall and lush and healthy and happy.

"Along comes a cottontail rabbit. She eats the green grass and goes back into the bush to make a nest. She pulls some fur from her breast, lines the nest carefully, and gives birth to her young. In a short while, the young rabbits are eating the green grass, and life is very good for cottontail rabbits."

Jack paused to see if anyone was paying attention. Everyone's eyes quickly left their feet to focus on his face. He continued on.

"Along comes a red fox. She is female, a vixen. And she has young of her own in an old woodchuck burrow on yonder hillside. Her pups are always hungry, begging for food. So, she must hunt very carefully to feed them. This she does. She comes upon the young rabbits and quickly kills two of them. She takes them back to her den, where she tears them into little pieces and feeds each of her pups. Now the little fox pups' bellies are full. They roll and tumble and play and growl in the springtime sun, and life is very good for the red fox family."

Lance interrupted the story. "Why'd she have to take two of the little rabbits? I'm getting cold sittin' here on this log!"

"'Cause her pups were hungry, Lance. She took enough to feed them all. When the getting is easy, all things do the same. It's natural." Jack clapped his hands together a few times.

Ellie said, "Lance, I guess we're all cold. But we're here as a family, so what your dad has to say is important, don't you think?"

Lance nodded. Jack took a breath and continued.

"Along comes a coyote. He says to himself, 'I don't like the red fox. I can smell them everywhere. I want this for my own hunting country.'" So the coyote chases the red foxes as far away as he can. Now life is very good for the coyote. He has no natural enemies this far south. The timber wolf doesn't come here to compete for hunting grounds. So, with the passing of time the coyote grows old. His teeth are dull, and his eyes become dim. He walks with a limp. He can no longer leap into the air to pounce on a meadow vole or field mouse.

So on the first warm day of late winter, when the sun melts the snow beneath a red cedar tree on a south-facing slope, the old coyote curls up and goes to sleep. He never wakes up. Now the rain and the wind, the sun and the moon, and the insects and the critters devour the coyote. In time, even its bones melt into the earth."

Jack stopped talking to glance at his family. The three of them looked like penguins all in a row, braced up against the cold winter wind. Yet all of their heads were turned in his direction. He continued his story.

"With the coming of spring, the green things again poke their heads from the earth. They're afraid at first. But with each passing day they gain courage. Soon the grasses stand tall and lush and healthy and happy. Along comes a cottontail rabbit. She eats the green grass and goes back into the brush to make a nest. She pulls some fur from her breast, lines the nest carefully, and gives birth to her young. In a short while, the young rabbits are eating the green grass, and life is very good for the cottontail rabbits. Of course, that's not the end of the story."

"Why not, Dad?" Katie piped up. "It ended just like it began, didn't it?"

"Sure did, honey. That's why it's called the circle of life. A perfect circle has no beginning, and it has no end. All things just keep happening over and over again, as long as all the travelers keep their place in the circle. However, if one species goes it will be sorely missed by all the fellow travelers," Jack replied.

He slapped his gloved hands together. "I've been moving my jaws for the last ten minutes, and that's about the only thing on me that ain't cold. Let's get moving, gang, aye?"

The little group got up, stomped their feet, and set off for the marsh. The sky was steel gray. It was beginning to snow again.

At the edge of the marsh were many brush piles, tops from trees the loggers had cut. Suddenly a white-tailed doe and last summer's fawns jumped from behind the brush. Their white tails bounced from side to side as they bounded away.

Lance shouted, "Why didn't you shoot 'em, Dad? It's deer season, ain't it?"

"Yup, it's deer season, but I've only got a small-game license. Can't be shooting everything we come across. Even with the right license we only kill as much as we can use—no more—so there's plenty left for other people and other years to come."

Jack thought for a moment. "Maybe next year I'll get a deer license. Lance, you're old enough to

Muskrat for Supper

take the hunter education course—you and I'll both carry a gun. The four of us could come out here and maybe, just maybe, get a deer. What do you think of that, Lance?"

"Cool, Dad, real cool."

Jack turned to glance at Katie. A smile slowly crossed her face.

Out on the frozen water, Jack untied the axe from the pack and swung it hard against the ice, chips flying out everywhere. No water came up through the place where he had chopped—the ice was safe to walk on in single file. Now they could begin setting their trapline.

When they came to the first muskrat house, Jack chopped a hole all the way through the ice about three feet from it. Water poured out of the hole. Jack used his boot to spread water around the house.

"Dad, why're you doing that?" Katie asked.

"You see how the water melts the snow? Now we can see if there are air bubbles frozen in the ice. Whenever there's a string of air bubbles, we know that the muskrats have been swimming there below the ice. They follow a sort of underwater trail in the ice, just like we follow roads and geese follow trails in the sky. Old-time trappers call these trails rat runs. The muskrat swims along on the bottom using his hind feet. Even in winter, the muskrat swims out several times a day to dig roots…cattails, arrowhead, and such. While swimming along, he gives off an air bubble from his lungs—that's what we see in the ice."

"There's a rat run, Dad," said Lance, pointing to a line of frozen air bubbles. Jack chopped a hole then got an arm-length glove from Lance's fanny pack. He swept the ice chips from the hole, knelt down, and felt around under the ice.

"We'll set one here."

Katie got a trap from the pack, and Ellie took it over to Jack, along with a peeled willow stick. They all gathered around Jack, who was still kneeling on the ice. He held the trap up for everyone to see.

"This is called a conibear trap," he explained. He squeezed the handle, or spring, of the trap and set the trigger, made of twin wires, in the center of the six-inch jaws. "The muskrat will swim along its underwater trail and into the trigger of the trap, which will then set off the jaws to clamp around the muskrat's body, killing the rat in a short time—about a minute or so. These are called body-gripping traps. One always wants to kill one of our fellow travelers as quickly as possible and for a good reason—it's humane. We don't want the animal to suffer. Remember, we're only hunting so that we might live ourselves and put the critter to good use. To waste a life is wrong." Jack shoved the willow through the trap spring and into the mud to hold it in place.

They spent the rest of the afternoon setting six more traps. Lance, Katie, Ellie, and Jack each took turns chopping holes, looking for rat runs, getting traps from the pack, and carrying willows. The sky darkened as an owl hooted in the distance. The adventurous trapper-hunters made their way back toward their camper, nestled under a large bare oak tree. Even without its leaves the tree seemed to offer shelter. Its dark limbs sharply contrasted against the cold grey evening sky. The wind was picking up. Again, the owl hooted.

The weary travelers stomped the snow off their boots and climbed inside the camper. They flopped

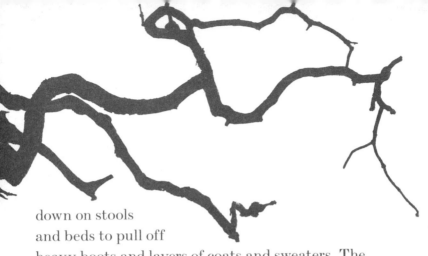

down on stools
and beds to pull off
heavy boots and layers of coats and sweaters. The
warmth of the gas furnace felt good.

After awhile Jack stood up. "Ellie, you and
Katie wash up and rest. Lance and I will make
supper." Lance gave his dad a sideways glance,
then reluctantly, with a groan, got up to help. In
short time, fried ham and potatoes, apple pie, and
plenty of hot chocolate took care of their hunger.

The family settled in to talk over the day's
adventures, but their eyes soon grew heavy. Still,
Lance had enough energy to ask one more question. "Dad, we hunted and trapped all day and we
didn't get a single thing. How come?"

"Son, there's a lot more to hunting and trapping than just killing something. What about

breathing all that cool clean air, seeing the fall of fresh snow, and all those animal tracks and the white-tail deer?"

"Yeah, and all the birds we heard...and we shared our lunch with one too," said Katie.

"What about the family just doing something together outdoors?" Ellie chimed in. "And how about this family going to bed now? I'm beat."

Lance had the last word. "I guess it was a neat day, but I'd still like to get something tomorrow."

As everyone drifted off to sleep, they could hear the great horned owl softly whispering its hunting call from its perch on the big oak tree, high above the little camper. The clouds were breaking and moonshadows played back and forth across the fresh snow.

Morning came fast for Ellie. After frying up some bacon and eggs, making toast, and pouring orange juice, she gave the wake-up call. "Breakfast is ready!"

After the morning meal, everyone bundled up in their warmest clothes, shouldered their packs, and hit the trail. The sun was just clearing the treetops…almost balancing there like a big orangish-yellow ball. The snow squeaked and squawked under their boots. Their breath looked like little puffs of smoke in the crisp morning air.

Here and there, deer tracks crossed yesterday's trail. The fox had been back too.

Ellie whispered, "Hold up, Jack," and pointed over toward a brush pile. They all went over to see. In a small circle were bits of fur and specks of blood. "Somebody had supper last night—looks like rabbit fur," said Ellie. Ellie, Katie, and Lance each took a turn looking closely at the kill. They all agreed that a rabbit had been eaten.

"What ate the rabbit?" Jack asked his kids.

"I think it was the owl we heard hooting above our camper last night!" Katie answered. "There aren't any tracks around here, and Lance said these marks in the snow are from its wing tips."

Jack was impressed. "Hey, that's some good detective work on your part. I'm very proud of you. If we're going to be outdoor people, we have to learn the ways of the creatures that live here."

They walked on. When they got close to the brush piles at the edge of the marsh, Jack raised his hand and they all stopped. "There's rabbit tracks leading to that pile," he whispered. Jack loaded his gun with two shells and moved quietly toward the pile, his gun on safety. Ellie, Katie, and Lance stood motionless.

When Jack got to the brush pile, he gave it a kick. As a quick as a flash, a rabbit burst forth, running at full speed. Jack snapped off the safety, shouldered the shotgun, swung the gun barrel along with the speed of the rabbit, saw a little space between the rabbit's head and the end of the barrel, and pulled the trigger. With the crack of the gun, a fountain of snow flew upward just behind the rabbit, urging it on even more quickly.

Without taking the gun from his shoulder, Jack quickly pumped another shell into the barrel— *click clack*. Once again he swung the barrel along with the rabbit and then past the rabbit's head. This time he saw more space between the rabbit's head and the end of the barrel when he pulled the trigger. The shot rang out and the rabbit rolled end over end, then lay quietly on its side in the powdery snow. Jack put his safety on again.

"You got 'im dad, you got 'im!" Lance hollered. He started to run toward the dead rabbit.

"Let it lie there, Lance," Jack said as he opened the action of his shotgun, double-checked the barrel to be sure the gun was empty, and set it securely against the brush pile.

The four hunters walked to where the rabbit lay. They stood in a circle around the rabbit looking down at it. "Please be quiet for a few moments," said Jack.

At first it was dead quiet. Then a blue jay called from afar. A squirrel barked from a treetop. A crow flew overhead. The north wind blew across the dead rabbit, sending its thick winter fur rippling back and forth. From a nearby branch, a chickadee sang its winter song, "chickadee-chickadee-dee-dee." Finally Jack spoke.

"When I was a kid back home on the farm, there was an old man who lived in a shack down by the creek. He taught my sister and me to hunt and fish and trap. He always said, 'Every time we take something from nature or nature gives us something, we should be grateful. We should always treat the natural things with respect and dignity.'"

Ellie got out a sharp knife, a rag, and a plastic bag from her pack. She picked up the rabbit and laid it belly side up on an oak stump. She took the knife and made a cut through the skin, around its back. Then she said, "Katie, grab the fur and pull toward the head. Lance, you pull toward the rear."

Jack took the axe and cut off the rabbit's feet and head. Now Ellie used the knife to cut the skinned carcass from the rear, up the belly, through the ribs. Next, she pulled all the insides out. Ellie rolled the rabbit about in the fresh snow to clean the blood off, then put it in a plastic bag along with plenty of snow and put the bag in the pack. They all washed their hands in the snow and dried their hands with the rag.

"Come on, partners, we've got traps to check!" Jack exclaimed. With that, the little group of explorers were off to the marsh. When they came to the first trap stake, Jack showed his daughter how to chop through the light coating of ice that had formed overnight. Then he gave Ellie the long rubber gloves and asked her to scoop the chips of ice from the hole. She then reached through the hole and felt around.

"Lance, pull up that willow trap stake," Jack instructed. A moment later, Ellie dragged a medium-sized muskrat up on top of the ice. It was stone dead.

The body-grip trap had caught the muskrat around the neck and ribs. It had died quickly, just as quickly as if an owl or mink had caught it. Jack squeezed the trap spring and removed the muskrat. He shook some of the water and mud off the rat and rolled and slid it around on the snow, wiping the mud and water from the muskrat's fur. He laid it down in a fresh patch of snow, and the family gathered around the muskrat in a circle. They stood there quietly, as they had with the rabbit. The afternoon sun shone and sparkled off the muskrat's dark brown fur. In the marsh, the north wind sang a different song than it had through the tree branches in the woods. Here, it used the dried stalks of wild rice, cattails, and bulrushes to make its music. All tangled and twisted and broken, they sang such a lovely, lonesome song for the family of hunter-trappers to enjoy.

The muskrat was placed carefully in Katie's pack, and they started off for the next trap stake. During the rest of the afternoon, they shared the trapline, their lunch, and their thoughts.

Toward evening, the family stopped at the edge of the marsh to skin their catch. They had taken three muskrats from the seven traps. It took them quite a while to skin all the muskrats because Jack and Ellie hadn't skinned any since their college days. The family cut off the hind legs from the skinned muskrats and put them in a plastic bag along with plenty of snow.

"Old Zeno—the trapper who lived in the shack by your grandpa's farm—called these muskrat saddles," Ellie explained. "Your dad and I enjoyed many a good meal of wild game in that old shack. Let's start a fire outside the camper tonight and cook up some rabbit and muskrat. How about it?"

Lance and Jack grinned. "Sounds great to us!"

Katie smiled a little but said nothing.

They watched the sun set behind the trees on the far side of the marsh. Jack put the muskrat pelts into his pack and placed what was left of their bodies, the hind legs had been removed for supper, on a stump.

"The fox and owls and all the other creatures will have muskrat for supper too,"

Jack said. "Then the circle of life will continue; nothing will be wasted."

They lifted their packs and trudged up the little wooded hill to the camper. Back at the trailer, they washed up, replaced damp clothes with dry, warm ones, and kicked back to enjoy hot apple cider with cinnamon sticks. Later, Ellie and Lance went outside and gathered dry sticks to light the fire. Katie and Jack cut up the rabbit and muskrat saddles, washed the meat, salted and peppered it, and wrapped it in some tinfoil with onions, celery, and green peppers. They went outside and joined Lance and Ellie, who were sitting on blocks of wood and staring into the crackling fire. Katie and Jack rounded up their own "chairs" and sat down next to their fellow travelers to wait and watch and think.

"I don't know why, but I just can't quit looking into the fire," Lance declared.

Without shifting his gaze from the flames, Jack answered, "I feel the same way, son. Always have. I guess most folks feel that way."

Ellie and Katie chimed in, "Sure enough."

"I think it's 'cause a fire comes from a living

thing, a tree," Ellie offered. "And the fire takes away the fear of uncertainty of darkness. It gives heat for cooking and to warm ourselves."

Katie added, "Just smelling the smoke makes me feel good. I love to follow the sparks. They seem to rise up to meet the stars...but they always disappear before they get there."

Soon the wood fire burned down to cooking coals. They put the tinfoil packages right in the glowing coals.

"You know, I never thought much about the circle of life before, but now it makes sense," Katie said. "One creature dies so another can live. As long as we take care of *all* of nature and leave *plenty* of plants and creatures for 'seed,' there will always be homes for the creatures and creatures for the homes." She looked up at Ellie, "Right, Mom?"

Ellie nodded. "That's right, Katie. We all have that responsibility."

Jack chuckled. "You know, Ellie, that could have been Old Zeno talking instead of Katie— only he'd 'ave called them critters instead of creatures." Ellie smiled at Jack.

Lance said, "Boy that stuff sure smells good. I'm hungry!"

Jack opened the tinfoil packages, stuck a fork into the meat, and said, "Supper is ready." Bread

and butter was served with the rabbit and muskrat. Katie bit hesitantly into the meat, chewing
slowly at first, but soon she was wolfing down the
tasty meal with the rest of the family.

After eating, Lance put one more piece of
wood on the coals, and a small fire was once again
burning. Jack stood up, so did Ellie, then Katie
and Lance. They all joined hands, forming a circle
around the fire. While they stood there quietly,
their puffs of breath seemed to mingle perfectly
with the campfire smoke as it curled upward into
the crisp, starry nighttime sky. On silent wings the
great horned owl drifted across the sky to land on
its perch high in the hunting tree above the campfire. The night hunter slowly looked around until
its eyes found the family circle below. The flickering fire shadows danced across the four tired but
very happy faces.

Somehow the circle of life seemed more com-
plete than it had just a day or two ago.

The Circle Widens

The girl smiles broadly at her parents. "That story makes me want to go camping. This fire sure is nice, but hot cocoa and sleeping out sounds fun. I'd love to hear the owls and see all the other birds!"

"Yeah, and it'd be neat to learn how to hunt," the boy says. "We'd be sure to only take what we need. Right, Mom?"

"Of course," Mom assures everyone.

"I bet we could live just like a river rat!" the boy exclaims.

Again, the river rat smiles kindly at the boy...

Muskrat for Supper

If a young person were to want to live like I have, on the river, my advice would be that they would need to lower their expectations in terms of finances. There is no way in the world that they could live a modern lifestyle. That's the first thing: you have to be realistic. However, if you wanted to live pretty much in financial poverty, that doesn't mean that you are poor. I always felt rich in a lot of ways: rich in outdoor experiences, rich in freedom, rich in my friends in nature. John Madson wrote a book on the Upper Mississippi called *Up on the River.* He interviewed quite a number of river rats many years back. He came to this definition of *river rat*: "A river rat is too crazy to freeze to death, too full of hot air to drown, and too ornery and independent to call anybody boss."

All of us answer to somebody, somehow, sometime. However, if you want to be a river rat, plan on working harder than you would for any regular job—no paid vacation, no sick days, no holidays. Yet, at the right time of the year, you can say, "I'm going to take the canoe and sit under a shade tree for the afternoon." So my advice would be to learn about the circle, learn as very much as possible—you have to know quite a bit just to survive, in terms of what is good and what is bad, how do critters live, where are they this time of year, how to fish, and all that sort of stuff. So, there is a lot to be learned.

I would start out as a part-timer. Evenings, weekends, or whenever. Save whatever you can for equipment to be purchased; you need canoes, you need fishing equipment. If you are going to fish commercially, you need setlines. They don't give those things away, you know. And you need traps if you are going to trap. So, it's admirable, and it seems like a romantic way to live—adventure-some—and I think it is; however, it isn't no Sunday school picnic, and these places are not parks. They are wild places.

One time, an old game warden named Jim Everson, the last of the old-time river wardens and a friend of mine, came by. I was sitting out by the tent camp, and I heard an airboat coming up through the swamp. (An airboat is a flat-bottom boat with an airplane engine on it, makes a lot of noise, goes over shallow water.) There weren't many back then, but the game warden had one, so I knew it was him. I was sitting on the steps by the tent camp, and Jim pulled in, crawled up alongside of me, and said, "What are you doing, Kenny?"

I said, "Well, I'm just swatting flies and mosquitoes, waiting for dark to set out some setlines for catfish." (That's a commercial way to catch catfish.)

He said, "The reason I'm here is because there's a teacher's workshop in Wabasha, Minnesota, this weekend for fifty-five teachers. Those of us at the Department of Natural Resources and the Fish and Wildlife folks are teaching them about the Upper Mississippi River. On Saturday night, there is going to be a banquet for those teachers." And he said, "I can't make it. I'm supposed to do a nature talk to those folks, and I'm wondering if you could?"

I said, "I should go? I never liked school. I never liked schoolteachers, and I would be surrounded by fifty-five of them. Right now, I'm not sure I like game wardens."

Jim Everson looked me right straight in the eye and said, "You are one of the most selfish, greedy people I have ever met in my life. All you do is take, take, take from nature."

I said, "What would I do there?"

He said, "Well, you come from a long line of

storytellers. Your grandmother who lived to be ninety-eight and a half—she was known as one of the best storytellers along the river. Go there and tell those folks some stories. Share something for a change." He said, "They might enjoy it, it might do you some good, and you get twenty-five dollars and a free meal."

I answered, "Okay, I'll go."

So, I went for all the wrong reasons. When I got there, I was as nervous as a long-tailed cat in a room full of rocking chairs, you know what I'm saying. Well, I got up and told some stories, and to my surprise, some teachers came and invited me to come to their schools to do the same for their students. Even more surprisingly, I said I would— and I did.

I found out the most peculiar paradox: if I were to see the great circle of life remain healthy and happy, the way I hoped to see it remain, I needed to give it away in order to keep it. If folks couldn't learn about it, they couldn't love and respect it. If you don't love and respect the circle, you won't take care of it. That's the way it is. That was about twenty years ago, and from that time on I've been doing it. I started out with easy talks, maybe four a year. It got to be state parks, wildlife bureaus, churches, ladies' groups, and civic clubs to where if I'm not doing a book tour, I am doing a hundred or more talks a year—about one every three days.

I was brought up to respect the circle; however, I still had that attitude that I had in the little country school—that schoolwork was for other people and I could get by without that. Sometimes I would take a few too many fish or something. What Everson taught me was that I was stealing from future generations, stealing from those who come behind me. I never really thought of it that way before.

I've met so many people from all over the world and all walks of life, and I have been very fortunate that they've seen fit to be kind to me— to treat me as an equal. Which I can't really ever be, because I'm playing catch-up.

I taught a college class, mind you, for several years. They called me adjunct professor. I loved that word, *adjunct* professor; I could "add junk" to the curriculum in a state university and get

paid for it! I had to give that up when this bad hip came along, and I had to have the hip replaced. I just wasn't physically able to come out here Saturday mornings and camp, and go home Sunday night, not four times a year. But who would have thought that? What a twist. You see, I don't know why that all happens. But I'm glad it does; it's a good new life. It sure is.

My uncles always used to say, "When you are young, you use your legs, and when you are old, you use your head." That is what I'm trying to do now. The days of me making a living as a river rat are over, physically, but I will never retire. What would I retire from? You need to have a job to retire. I enjoy what I'm doing, so I'll keep a-going.

The story of Lance and Katie and their parents does not end here—and neither does your story. Their family has only begun to share outdoor experiences, along with their feelings, attitudes, and values toward those experiences.

Without a doubt, the family will also share those things with friends and others, just like you will when you leave here, and each time you go out exploring. And as time passes, Lance and Katie (and you) will include their own families as well. This is how the circle widens.

Once again, education through outdoor experiences evokes feelings. Those feelings produce attitudes and values. Attitudes and values, in turn, create behavior—how we behave toward the great circle of life.

For as long as the robin sings, and the green

grass grows with the coming of spring, and lovely wildflowers send their sweet fragrances to waft upon a gentle summer breeze; as long as the white-tailed deer drifts through the autumn woods like a dark shadow and the turtle sleeps away the winter in that black, boot-sucking Mississippi mud, I shall remain grateful to you kids for allowing this old river rat to share some of my life's thoughts and stories. And for taking good care of the wild things and the wild places. They need you.

Thank you from the bottom of my heart!

About the Author

Kenny Salwey is the last of a breed of men whose lifestyle has all but disappeared in this fast-paced, high-tech digital world. For thirty years, this weathered woodsman eked out a living on the Mississippi River, running a trapline, hiring out as a river guide, digging and selling roots and herbs, and eating the food he hunted and fished. Today, Salwey is a master storyteller, environmental educator, keynote speaker, nature writer, and advocate for the Upper Mississippi River. He has presented his true-life adventures and words of natural world wisdom to both adult and young audiences across the Upper Midwest. By sharing his experiences, his hard-learned respect for the Mississippi River, and his love of the natural world, Salwey hopes to inspire his audiences to protect this precious and fragile ecosystem.